ROGUES IN THE HOUSE

BY

ROBERT E. HOWARD

British Library Cataloguing-in-Publication Data
A catalogue record for this book is available from the
British Library

Contents

Robert E. Howard

Robert Ervin Howard was born in Peaster, Texas in 1906. During his youth, his family moved between a variety of Texan boomtowns, and Howard – a bookish and somewhat introverted child – was steeped in the violent myths and legends of the Old South. Although he loved reading and learning, Howard developed a distinctly Texan, hardboiled outlook on the world. He became a passionate fan of boxing, taking it up at an amateur level, and from the age of nine began to write adventure tales of semi-historical bloodshed. In 1919, when Howard was thirteen, his family moved to the Central Texas hamlet of Cross Plains, where he would stay for the rest of his life.

At fifteen Howard began to read the pulp magazines of the day, and to write more seriously. The December 1922 issue of his high school newspaper featured two of his stories, 'Golden Hope Christmas' and 'West is West'. In 1924 he sold his first piece – a short caveman tale titled 'Spear and Fang' – for $16 to the not-yet-famous *Weird Tales* magazine. He published with the magazine regularly over the next few years. 1929 was a breakout year for Howard, in that the 23-year-old writer began to sell to other magazines, such as *Ghost Stories* and *Argosy*, both of whom had previously sent him hundreds of rejection slips. In 1930, he began a correspondence with weird fiction master H. P. Lovecraft which ran up to his death six years later, and is regarded as one of the great correspondence cycles in all of fantasy literature.

It was partly due to Lovecraft's encouragement that Howard created his most famous character, Conan the Cimmerian. Conan – a barbarian-turned-King during the Hyborian Age, a mythical period of some 12,000 years ago – featured in seventeen *Weird Tales* stories between 1933 and 1936, and is now regarded as having spawned the 'sword and sorcery' genre, making Howard's influence on fantasy literature comparable to that of J. R. R. Tolkien's. The Conan stories have since been adapted many times, most famously in the series of films starring Arnold Schwarzenegger.

Howard was enjoying an all-time high in sales by the beginning of 1936, but he was also deeply upset by the ill health of his mother, who had fallen into a coma. On the morning of June 11, 1936, he asked an attending nurse whether she would ever recover, and the nurse replied negatively. Howard walked to his car, parked outside the family home in Cross Plains, and shot himself. He died eight hours later, aged just thirty.

CHAPTER I

At a court festival, Nabonidus, the Red Priest, who was the real ruler of the city, touched Murilo, the young aristocrat, courteously on the arm. Murilo turned to meet the priest's enigmatic gaze, and to wonder at the hidden meaning therein. No words passed between them, but Nabonidus bowed and handed Murilo a small gold cask. The young nobleman, knowing that Nabonidus did nothing without reason, excused himself at the first opportunity and returned hastily to his chamber. There he opened the cask and found within a human ear, which he recognized by a peculiar scar upon it. He broke into a profuse sweat and was no longer in doubt about the meaning in the Red Priest's glance.

But Murilo, for all his scented black curls and foppish apparel was no weakling to bend his neck to the knife without a struggle. He did not know whether Nabonidus was merely playing with him or giving him a chance to go into voluntary exile, but the fact that he was still alive and at liberty proved that he was to be given at least a few hours, probably for meditation. However, he needed no meditation for decision; what he needed was a tool. And Fate furnished that tool, working among the dives and brothels of the squalid quarters even while the young nobleman shivered and pondered in the part of the city occupied by the purple-towered marble and ivory palaces of the aristocracy.

There was a priest of Anu whose temple, rising at the fringe of the slum district, was the scene of more than devotions. The priest was fat and full-fed, and he was at once a fence for stolen articles and a spy for the police. He worked a thriving trade both ways, because the district on which he bordered was the Maze, a tangle of muddy, winding alleys and sordid dens, frequented by the bolder thieves in the kingdom. Daring above all were a Gunderman deserter from the mercenaries and a barbaric Cimmerian. Because of the priest of Anu, the Gunderman was taken and hanged in the market square. But the Cimmerian fled, and learning in devious ways of the priest's treachery, he entered the temple of Anu by night and cut off the priest's head. There followed a great turmoil in the city, but the search for the killer proved fruitless until a woman betrayed him to the authorities and led a captain of the guard and his squad to the hidden chamber where the barbarian lay drunk.

Waking to stupefied but ferocious life when they seized him, he disemboweled the captain, burst through his assailants, and would have escaped but for the liquor that still clouded his senses. Bewildered and half blinded, he missed the open door in his headlong flight and dashed his head against the stone wall so terrifically that he knocked himself senseless. When he came to, he was in the strongest dungeon in the city, shackled to the wall with chains not even his barbaric thews could break.

To this cell came Murilo, masked and wrapped in a wide black cloak. The Cimmerian surveyed him with interest, thinking him the executioner sent to dispatch him. Murilo set him at rights and regarded him with no less interest. Even in the dim light of the dungeon, with his limbs loaded with chains, the primitive power of the man was evident. His mighty body and thick-muscled limbs combined the strength of a grizzly with the quickness of a panther. Under his tangled black mane his blue eyes blazed with unquenchable savagery.

"Would you like to live?" asked Murilo. The barbarian grunted, new interest glinting in his eyes.

"If I arrange for your escape, will you do a favor for me?" the aristocrat asked.

The Cimmerian did not speak, but the intentness of his gaze answered for him.

"I want you to kill a man for me."

"Who?"

Murilo's voice sank to a whisper. "Nabonidus, the king's priest!"

The Cimmerian showed no sign of surprise or perturbation. He had none of the fear or reverence for authority that civilization instills in men. King or beggar, it was all one to him. Nor did he ask why Murilo had come to him, when the quarters were full of cutthroats outside prisons.

"When am I to escape?" he demanded.

"Within the hour. There is but one guard in this part of the dungeon at night. He can be bribed; he *has* been bribed. See, here are the keys to your chains. I'll remove them and, after I have been gone an hour, the guard, Athicus, will unlock the door to your cell. You will bind him with strips torn from your tunic; so when he is found, the authorities will think you were rescued from the outside and will not suspect him. Go at once to the house of the Red Priest and kill him. Then go to the Rats' Den, where a man will meet you and give you a pouch of gold and a horse. With those you can escape from the city and flee the country."

"Take off these cursed chains now," demanded the Cimmerian. "And have the guard bring me food. By Crom, I have lived on moldy bread and water for a whole day, and I am nigh to famishing."

"It shall be done; but remember — you are not to escape until I have had time to reach my home."

Freed of his chains, the barbarian stood up and stretched his heavy arms, enormous in the gloom of the dungeon. Murilo again felt that if any man in the world could accomplish the task he had set, this Cimmerian could. With a few repeated instructions he left the prison, first directing Athicus to take a platter of beef and ale in to the prisoner.

He knew he could trust the guard, not only because of the money he had paid, but also because of certain information he possessed regarding the man.

When he returned to his chamber, Murilo was in full control of his fears. Nabonidus would strike through the king — of that he was certain. And since the royal guardsmen were not knocking at his door, it was certain that the priest had said nothing to the king, so far. Tomorrow he would speak, beyond a doubt — if he lived to see tomorrow.

Murilo believed the Cimmerian would keep faith with him. Whether the man would be able to carry out his purpose remained to be seen. Men had attempted to assassinate the Red Priest before, and they had died in hideous and nameless ways. But they had been products of the cities of men, lacking the wolfish instincts of the barbarian. The instant that Murilo, turning the gold cask with its severed ear in his hands, had learned through his secret channels that the Cimmerian had been captured, he had seen a solution of his problem.

In his chamber again, he drank a toast to the man, whose name was Conan, and to his success that night. And while he was drinking, one of his spies brought him the news that Athicus had been arrested and thrown into prison. The Cimmerian had not escaped.

Murilo felt his blood turn to ice again. He could see in this twist of fate only the sinister hand of Nabonidus, and an eery obsession began to grow on him that the Red Priest was more than human — a sorcerer who read the minds of his victims and pulled strings on which they danced like puppets. With despair came desperation. Girding a sword beneath his black cloak, he left his house by a hidden way and hurried through the deserted streets. It was just at midnight when he came to the house of Nabonidus, looming blackly among the walled gardens that separated it from the surrounding estates.

The wall was high but not impossible to negotiate. Nabonidus did not put his trust in mere barriers of stone. It was what was inside the wall that was to be feared. What these things were Murilo did not know precisely. He knew there was at least a huge savage dog that roamed the gardens and had on occasion torn an intruder to pieces as a hound rends a rabbit. What else there might be he did not care to conjecture. Men who had been allowed to enter the house on brief, legitimate business, reported that Nabonidus dwelt among rich furnishings, yet simply, attended by a surprisingly small number of servants. Indeed, they mentioned only one as having been visible — a tall, silent man called Joka. Some one else, presumably a slave, had been heard moving about in the recesses of the house, but this person no one had ever seen. The greatest mystery of the mysterious house was Nabonidus himself, whose power of intrigue and grasp on international politics had made him the strongest man in the kingdom. People, chancellor and king moved puppetlike on the strings he worked.

Murilo scaled the wall and dropped down into the gardens, which were expanses of shadow, darkened by clumps of shrubbery and waving foliage. No light shone in the windows of the house, which loomed so blackly among the trees. The young nobleman stole stealthily yet swiftly through the shrubs. Momentarily he expected to hear the baying of the great dog and to see its giant body hurtle through the shadows. He doubted the effectiveness of his sword against such an attack, but he did not hesitate. As well die beneath the fangs of a beast as of the headsman.

He stumbled over something bulky and yielding. Bending close in the dim starlight, he made out a limp shape on the ground. It was the dog that guarded the gardens, and it was dead. Its neck was broken and it bore what seemed to be the marks of great fangs. Murilo felt that no human being had done this. The beast had met a monster more savage than itself. Murilo glared nervously at the cryptic masses of bush and shrub; then with a shrug of his shoulders, he approached the silent house.

The first door he tried proved to be unlocked. He entered warily, sword in hand, and found himself in a long, shadowy hallway dimly illuminated by a light that gleamed through the hangings at the other end. Complete silence hung over the whole house. Murilo glided along the hall and halted to peer through the hangings. He looked into a lighted room, over the windows of which velvet curtains were drawn so closely as to allow no beam to shine through. The room was empty, in so far as human life was concerned, but it had a grisly occupant, nevertheless: in the midst of a wreckage of furniture and torn hangings that told of a fearful struggle, lay the body of a man. The form lay on its belly, but the head was twisted about so that the chin rested behind a shoulder. The features, contorted into an awful grin, seemed to leer at the horrified nobleman.

For the first time that night, Murilo's resolution wavered. He cast an uncertain glance back the way he had come. Then the memory of the headsman's block and axe steeled him, and he crossed the room, swerving to avoid the grinning horror sprawled in its midst. Though he had never seen the man before, he knew from former descriptions that it was Joka, Nabonidus' saturnine servant.

He peered through a curtained door into a broad circular chamber, banded by a gallery half-way between the polished floor and the lofty ceiling. This chamber was furnished as if for a king. In the midst of it stood an ornate mahogany table, loaded with vessels of wine and rich viands. And Murilo stiffened. In a great chair whose broad back was toward him, he saw a figure whose habiliments were familiar. He glimpsed an arm in a red sleeve resting on the arm of the chair; the head, clad in the familiar scarlet hood of the gown, was bent forward as if in meditation. Just so had Murilo seen Nabonidus sit a hundred times in the royal court.

Cursing the pounding of his own heart, the young nobleman stole across the chamber, sword extended, his whole frame poised for the thrust. His prey did not move, nor seem to hear his cautious advance. Was the Red Priest asleep, or was it a corpse which slumped in that great chair? The length of a single stride separated Murilo from his enemy, when suddenly the man in the chair rose and faced him.

The blood went suddenly from Murilo's features. His sword fell from his fingers and rang on the polished floor. A terrible cry broke from his livid lips; it was followed by the thud of a falling body. Then once more silence reigned over the house of the Red Priest.

CHAPTER II

Shortly after Murilo left the dungeon where Conan the Cimmerian was confined, Athicus brought the prisoner a platter of food which included, among other things, a huge joint of beef and a tankard of ale. Conan fell to voraciously, and Athicus made a final round of the cells, to see that all was in order, and that none should witness the pretended prison break. It was while he was so occupied that a squad of guardsmen marched into the prison and placed him under arrest. Murilo had been mistaken when he assumed this arrest denoted discovery of Conan's planned escape. It was another matter; Athicus had become careless in his dealings with the underworld, and one of his past sins had caught up with him.

Another jailer took his place, a stolid, dependable creature whom no amount of bribery could have shaken from his duty. He was unimaginative, but he had an exalted idea of the importance of his job.

After Athicus had been marched away to be formally arraigned before a magistrate, this jailer made the rounds of the cell as a matter of routine. As he passed that of Conan, his sense of propriety was shocked and outraged to see the prisoner free of his chains and in the act of gnawing the last shreds of meat from a huge beefbone. The jailer was so upset that he made the mistake of entering the cell alone, without calling guards from the other parts of the prison. It was his first mistake in the line of duty, and his last. Conan brained him with the beef bone, took his poniard and his keys, and made a leisurely departure. As Murilo had said, only one guard was on duty there at night. The Cimmerian passed himself outside the walls by means of the keys he had taken and presently emerged into the outer air, as free as if Murilo's plan had been successful.

In the shadows of the prison walls, Conan paused to decide his next course of action. It occurred to him that since he had escaped through his own actions, he owed nothing to Murilo; yet it had been the young nobleman who had removed his chains and had the food sent to him, without either of which his escape would have been impossible. Conan decided that he was indebted to Murilo and, since he was a man who discharged his obligations eventually, he determined to carry out his promise to the young aristocrat. But first he had some business of his own to attend to.

He discarded his ragged tunic and moved off through the night naked but for a loincloth. As he went he fingered the poniard he had captured — a murderous weapon with a broad, double-edged blade nineteen inches long. He slunk along alleys and shadowed plazas until he came to the district which was his destination — the Maze. Along its labyrinthian ways he went with the certainty of familiarity. It was indeed a maze of black alleys and enclosed courts and devious ways; of furtive sounds, and stenches. There was no paving on the streets; mud and filth mingled in an unsavory mess. Sewers were unknown; refuse was dumped into the alleys to form reeking heaps and puddles. Unless a man walked with care he was likely to lose his footing and plunge waist-deep into nauseous pools. Nor was it uncommon to stumble over a corpse lying with its throat cut or its head knocked in, in the mud. Honest folk shunned the Maze with good reason.

Conan reached his destination without being seen, just as one he wished fervently to meet was leaving it. As the Cimmerian slunk into the courtyard below, the girl who had sold him to the police was taking leave of her new lover in a chamber one flight up. This young thug, her door closed behind him, groped his way down a creaking flight of stairs, intent on his own meditations, which, like those of most of the denizens of the Maze, had to do with the unlawful acquirement of property. Part-way down the stairs, he halted suddenly, his hair standing up. A vague bulk crouched in the darkness before him, a pair of eyes blazed like the eyes of a hunting beast. A beastlike snarl was the last thing he heard in life, as the monster lurched against him and a keen blade ripped through his belly. He gave one gasping cry and slumped down limply on the stairway.

The barbarian loomed above him for an instant, ghoul-like, his eyes burning in the gloom. He knew the sound was heard, but the people in the Maze were careful to attend to their own business. A death cry on darkened stairs was nothing unusual. Later, some one would venture to investigate, but only after a reasonable lapse of time.

Conan went up the stairs and halted at a door he knew well of old. It was fastened within, but his blade passed between the door and the jamb and lifted the bar. He stepped inside, closing the door after him, and faced the girl who had betrayed him to the police.

The wench was sitting cross-legged in her shift on her unkempt bed. She turned white and stared at him as if at a ghost. She had heard the cry from the stairs, and she saw the red stain on the poniard in his hand. But she was too filled with terror on her own account to waste any time lamenting the evident fate of her lover. She began to beg for her life, almost incoherent with terror. Conan did not reply; he merely stood and glared at her with his burning eyes, testing the edge of his poniard with a callused thumb.

At last he crossed the chamber, while she cowered back against the wall, sobbing frantic pleas for mercy. Grasping her yellow locks with no gentle hand, he dragged her off the bed. Thrusting his blade in the sheath, he tucked his squirming captive under his left arm and strode to the window. As in most houses of that type, a ledge encircled each story, caused by the continuance of the window ledges. Conan kicked the window open and stepped out on that narrow band. If any had been near or awake, they would have witnessed the bizarre sight of a man moving carefully along the ledge, carrying a kicking, half-naked wench under his arm. They would have been no more puzzled than the girl.

Reaching the spot he sought, Conan halted, gripping the wall with his free hand. Inside the building rose a sudden clamor, showing that the body had at last been discovered. His captive whimpered and twisted, renewing her importunities. Conan glanced down into the muck and slime of the alleys below; he listened briefly to the clamor inside and the pleas of the wench; then he dropped her with great accuracy into a cesspool. He enjoyed her kickings and flounderings and the concentrated venom of her profanity for a few seconds, and even allowed himself a low rumble of laughter. Then he lifted his head, listened to the growing tumult within the building, and decided it was time for him to kill Nabonidus.

CHAPTER III

It was a reverberating clang of metal that roused Murilo. He groaned and struggled dazedly to a sitting position. About him all was silence and darkness, and for an instant he was sickened with the fear that he was blind. Then he remembered what had gone before, and his flesh crawled. By the sense of touch he found that he was lying on a floor of evenly joined stone slabs. Further groping discovered a wall of the same material. He rose and leaned against it, trying in vain to orient himself. That he was in some sort of a prison seemed certain, but where and how long he was unable to guess. He remembered dimly a clashing noise and wondered if it had been the iron door of his dungeon closing on him, or if it betokened the entrance of an executioner.

At this thought he shuddered profoundly and began to feel his way along the wall. Momentarily he expected to encounter the limits of his prison, but after a while he came to the conclusion that he was travelling down a corridor. He kept to the wall, fearful of pits of other traps, and was presently aware of something near him in the blackness. He could see nothing, but either his ears had caught a stealthy sound, or some subconscious sense warned him. He stopped short, his hair standing on end; as surely as he lived, he felt the presence of some living creature crouching in the darkness in front of him.

He thought his heart would stop when a voice hissed in a barbaric accent: “Murilo! Is it you?”

“Conan!” Limp from the reaction, the young nobleman groped in the darkness, and his hands encountered a pair of great naked shoulders.

“A good thing I recognized you,” grunted the barbarian. “I was about to stick you like a fattened pig.”

“Where are we, in Mitra’s name?”

“In the pits under the Red Priest’s house; but why—”

“What is the time?”

“Not long after midnight.”

Murilo shook his head, trying to assemble his scattered wits.

“What are you doing here?” demanded the Cimmerian.

“I came to kill Nabonidus. I heard they had changed the guard at your prison—”

“They did,” growled Conan. “I broke the new jailer’s head and walked out. I would have been here hours agone, but I had some personal business to attend to. Well, shall we hunt for Nabonidus?”

Murilo shuddered. “Conan, we are in the house of the archfiend! I came seeking a human enemy; I found a hairy devil out of hell!”

Conan grunted uncertainly; fearless as a wounded tiger as far as human foes were concerned, he had all the superstitious dreads of the primitive.

"I gained access to the house," whispered Murilo, as if the darkness were full of listening ears. "In the outer gardens I found Nabonidus' dog mauled to death. Within the house I came upon Joka, the servant. His neck had been broken. Then I saw Nabonidus himself seated in his chair, clad in his accustomed garb. At first I thought he, too, was dead. I stole up to stab him. He rose and faced me. God!" The memory of that horror struck the young nobleman momentarily speechless as he re-lived that awful instant.

"Conan," he whispered, "it was no *man* that stood before me! In body and posture it was not unlike a man, but from the scarlet hood of the priest grinned a face of madness and nightmare! It was covered with black hair, from which small pig-like eyes glared redly; its nose was flat, with great flaring nostrils; its loose lips writhed back, disclosing huge yellow fangs, like the teeth of a dog. The hands that hung from the scarlet sleeves were misshapen and likewise covered with black hair. All this I saw in one glance, and then I was overcome with horror; my senses left me and I swooned."

"What then?" muttered the Cimmerian uneasily.

"I recovered consciousness only a short time ago; the monster must have thrown me into these pits. Conan, I have suspected that Nabonidus was not wholly human! He is a demon — a were-thing! By day he moves among humanity in the guise of men, and by night he takes on his true aspect."

"That's evident," answered Conan. "Everyone knows there are men who take the form of wolves at will. But why did he kill his servants?"

"Who can delve the mind of a devil?" replied Murilo. "Our present interest is in getting out of this place. Human weapons cannot harm a were-man. How did you get in here?"

"Through the sewer. I reckoned on the gardens being guarded. The sewers connect with a tunnel that lets into these pits. I thought to find some door leading up into the house unbolted."

"Then let us escape by the way you came!" exclaimed Murilo. "To the devil with it! Once out of this snake-den, we'll take our chances with the king's guardsmen and risk a flight from the city. Lead on!"

"Useless," grunted the Cimmerian. "The way to the sewers is barred. As I entered the tunnel, an iron grille crashed down from the roof. If I had not moved quicker than a flash of lightning, its spearheads would have pinned me to the floor like a worm. When I tried to lift it, it wouldn't move. An elephant couldn't shake it. Nor could anything bigger than a rabbit squirm between the bars."

Murilo cursed, an icy hand playing up and down his spine. He might have known Nabonidus would not leave any entrance into his house unguarded. Had Conan not possessed the steel-spring quickness of a wild thing, that falling portcullis would have skewered him. Doubtless his walking through the tunnel had sprung some hidden catch that released it from the roof. As it was, both were trapped living.

"There's but one thing to do," said Murilo, sweating profusely. "That's to search for some other exit; doubtless they're all set with traps, but we have no other choice."

The barbarian grunted agreement, and the companions began groping their way at random down the corridor. Even at that moment, something occurred to Murilo.

"How did you recognize me in this blackness?" he demanded.

"I smelled the perfume you put on your hair, when you came to my cell," answered Conan. "I smelled it again a while ago, when I was crouching in the dark and preparing to rip you open."

Murilo put a lock of his black hair to his nostrils; even so the scent was barely apparent to his civilized senses, and he realized how keen must be the organs of the barbarian.

Instinctively his hand went to his scabbard as they groped onward, and he cursed to find it empty. At that moment a faint glow became apparent ahead of them, and presently they came to a sharp bend in the corridor, about which the light filtered grayly. Together they peered around the corner, and Murilo, leaning against his companion, felt his huge frame stiffen. The young nobleman had also seen it — the body of a man, half naked, lying limply in the corridor beyond the bend, vaguely illumined by a radiance which seemed to emanate from a broad silver disk on the farther wall. A strange familiarity about the recumbent figure, which lay face down, stirred Murilo with inexplicable and monstrous conjectures. Motioning the Cimmerian to follow him, he stole forward and bent above the body. Overcoming a certain repugnance, he grasped it and turned it on its back. An incredulous oath escaped him; the Cimmerian grunted explosively.

"Nabonidus! The Red Priest!" ejaculated Murilo, his brain a dizzy vortex of whirling amazement. "Then who — what — ?"

The priest groaned and stirred. With catlike quickness Conan bent over him, poniard poised above his heart. Murilo caught his wrist.

"Wait! Don't kill him yet—"

"Why not?" demanded the Cimmerian. "He has cast off his were-guise, and sleeps. Will you awaken him to tear us to pieces?"

"No, wait!" urged Murilo, trying to collect his jumbled wits. "Look! He is not sleeping — see that great blue welt on his shaven temple? He has been knocked senseless. He may have been lying here for hours."

"I thought you swore you saw him in beastly shape in the house above," said Conan.

"I did! Or else — he's coming to! Keep back your blade, Conan; there is a mystery here even darker than I thought. I must have words with this priest, before we kill him."

Nabonidus lifted a hand vaguely to his bruised temple, mumbled, and opened his eyes. For an instant they were blank and empty of intelligence; then life came back to them with a jerk, and he sat up, staring at the companions. Whatever terrific jolt had temporarily addled his razor-keen brain, it was functioning with its accustomed vigor again. His eyes shot swiftly about him, then came back to rest on Murilo's face.

"You honor my poor house, young sir," he laughed coolly, glancing at the great figure that loomed behind the young nobleman's shoulder. "You have brought a bravo, I see. Was your sword not sufficient to sever the life of my humble self?"

"Enough of this," impatiently returned Murilo. "How long have you lain here?"

"A peculiar question to put to a man just recovering consciousness," answered the priest. "I do not know what time it now is. But it lacked an hour or so of midnight when I was set upon."

"Then who is it that masquerades in your own gown in the house above?" demanded Murilo.

"That will be Thak," answered Nabonidus, ruefully fingering his bruises. "Yes, that will be Thak. And in my own gown? The dog!"

Conan, who comprehended none of this, stirred restlessly, and growled something in his own tongue. Nabonidus glanced at him whimsically.

"Your bully's knife yearns for my heart, Murilo," he said. "I thought you might be wise enough to take my warning and leave the city."

"How was I to know that was to be granted me?" returned Murilo. "At any rate, my interests are here."

"You are in good company with that cutthroat," murmured Nabonidus. "I had suspected you for some time. That was why I caused that pallid court secretary to disappear. Before he died he told me many things, among others the name of the young nobleman who bribed him to filch state secrets, which the nobleman in turn sold to rival powers. Are you not ashamed of yourself, Murilo, you white-handed thief?"

"I have no more cause for shame than you, you vulture-hearted plunderer," answered Murilo promptly. "You exploit a whole kingdom for your personal greed; and, under the guise of disinterested statesmanship, you swindle the king, beggar the rich, oppress the poor, and sacrifice the whole future of the nation for your ruthless ambition. You are no more than a fat hog with his snout in the trough. You are a greater thief than I am. This Cimmerian is the most honest man of the three of us, because he steals and murders openly."

"Well, then, we are all rogues together," agreed Nabonidus equably. "And what now? My life?"

"When I saw the ear of the secretary that had disappeared, I knew I was doomed," said Murilo abruptly, "and I believed you would invoke the authority of the king. Was I right?"

"Quite so," answered the priest. "A court secretary is easy to do away with, but you are a bit too prominent. I had intended telling the king a jest about you in the morning."

"A jest that would have cost me my head," muttered Murilo. "Then the king is unaware of my foreign enterprises?"

"As yet," sighed Nabonidus. "And now, since I see your companion has his knife, I fear that jest will never be told."

"You should know how to get out of these rat-dens," said Murilo. "Suppose I agree to spare your life. Will you help us to escape, and swear to keep silent about my thievery?"

"When did a priest keep an oath?" complained Conan, comprehending the trend of the conversation. "Let me cut his throat; I want to see what color his blood is. They say in the Maze that his heart is black, so his blood must be black, too—"

"Be quiet," whispered Murilo. "If he does not show us the way out of these pits, we may rot here. Well, Nabonidus, what do you say?"

"What does a wolf with his leg in the trap say?" laughed the priest. "I am in your power, and, if we are to escape, we must aid one another. I swear, if we survive this adventure, to forget all your shifty dealings. I swear by the soul of Mitra!"

"I am satisfied," muttered Murilo. "Even the Red Priest would not break that oath. Now to get out of here. My friend here entered by way of the tunnel, but a grille fell behind him and blocked the way. Can you cause it to be lifted?"

"Not from these pits," answered the priest. "The control lever is in the chamber above the tunnel. There is only one other way out of these pits, which I will show you. But tell me, how did you come here?"

Murilo told him in a few words, and Nabonidus nodded, rising stiffly. He limped down the corridor, which here widened into a sort of vast chamber, and approached the distant silver disk. As they advanced the light increased, though it never became anything but a dim shadowy radiance. Near the disk they saw a narrow stair leading upward.

"That is the other exit," said Nabonidus. "And I strongly doubt if the door at the head is bolted. But I have an idea that he who would go through that door had better cut his own throat first. Look into the disk."

What had seemed a silver plate was in reality a great mirror set in the wall. A confusing system of copperlike tubes jutted out from the wall above it, bending down toward it at right angles. Glancing into these tubes, Murilo saw a bewildering array of smaller mirrors. He turned his attention to the larger mirror in the wall, and ejaculated in amazement. Peering over his shoulder, Conan grunted.

They seemed to be looking through a broad window into a well-lighted chamber. There were broad mirrors on the walls, with velvet hangings between; there were silken couches, chairs of ebony and ivory, and curtained doorways leading off from the chamber. And before one doorway which was not curtained, sat a bulky black object that contrasted grotesquely with the richness of the chamber.

Murilo felt his blood freeze again as he looked at the horror which seemed to be staring directly into his eyes. Involuntarily he recoiled from the mirror, while Conan thrust his head truculently forward, till his jaws almost touched the surface, growling some threat or defiance in his own barbaric tongue.

"In Mitra's name, Nabonidus," gasped Murilo, shaken, "what is it?"

"That is Thak," answered the priest, caressing his temple. "Some would call him an ape, but he is almost as different from a real ape as he is different from a real man. His people dwell far to the east, in the mountains that fringe the eastern frontiers of Zamora. There are not many of them; but, if they are not exterminated, I believe they will become human beings in perhaps a hundred thousand years. They are in the formative stage; they are neither apes, as their remote ancestors were, nor men, as their remote descendants may be. They dwell in the high crags of well-nigh inaccessible mountains, knowing nothing of fire or the making of shelter or garments, or the use of weapons. Yet they have a language of a sort, consisting mainly of grunts and clicks.

"I took Thak when he was a cub, and he learned what I taught him much more swiftly and thoroughly than any true animal could have done. He was at once bodyguard and servant. But I forgot that being partly a man, he could not be submerged into a mere shadow of myself, like a true animal. Apparently his semi-brain retained impressions of hate, resentment, and some sort of bestial ambition of its own.

"At any rate, he struck when I least expected it. Last night he appeared to go suddenly mad. His actions had all the appearance of bestial insanity, yet I know that they must have been the result of long and careful planning.

"I heard a sound of fighting in the garden, and going to investigate — for I believed it was yourself, being dragged down by my watchdog — I saw Thak emerge from the shrubbery dripping with blood. Before I was aware of his intention, he sprang at me with an awful scream and struck me senseless. I remember no more, but can only surmise that, following some whim of his semi-human brain, he stripped me of my gown and cast me still living into the pits — for what reason, only the gods can guess. He must have killed the dog when he came from the garden, and after he struck me down, he evidently killed Joka, as you saw the man lying dead in the house. Joka would have come to my aid, even against Thak, who he always hated."

Murilo stared in the mirror at the creature which sat with such monstrous patience before the closed door. He shuddered at the sight of the great black hands, thickly grown with hair that was almost furlike. The body was thick, broad, and stooped. The unnaturally wide shoulders had burst the scarlet gown, and on these shoulders Murilo noted the same thick growth of black hair. The face peering from the scarlet hood was utterly bestial, and yet Murilo realized that Nabonidus spoke truth when he said that Thak was not wholly a beast. There was something in the red murky eyes, something in the creature's clumsy posture, something in the whole appearance of the thing that set it apart from the truly animal. That monstrous body housed a brain and soul that were just budding awfully into something vaguely human. Murilo stood aghast as he recognized a faint and hideous kinship between his kind and that squatting monstrosity, and he was nauseated by a fleeting realization of the abysses of bellowing bestiality up through which humanity had painfully toiled.

"Surely he sees us," muttered Conan. "Why does he not charge us? He could break this window with ease."

Murilo realized that Conan supposed the mirror to be a window through which they were looking.

"He does not see us," answered the priest. "We are looking into the chamber above us. That door that Thak is guarding is the one at the head of these stairs. It is simply an arrangement of mirrors. Do you see those mirrors on the walls? They transmit the reflection of the room into these tubes, down which other mirrors carry it to reflect it at last on an enlarged scale in this great mirror."

Murilo realized that the priest must be centuries ahead of his generation, to perfect such an invention; but Conan put it down to witchcraft and troubled his head no more about it.

"I constructed these pits for a place of refuge as well as a dungeon," the priest was saying. "There are times when I have taken refuge here and, through these mirrors, watched doom fall upon those who sought me with ill intent."

"But why is Thak watching that door?" demanded Murilo.

"He must have heard the falling of the grating in the tunnel. It is connected with bells in the chambers above. He knows someone is in the pits, and he is waiting for him to come up the stairs. Oh, he has learned well the lessons I taught him. He has seen what happened to men who come through that door, when I tugged at the rope that hangs on yonder wall, and he waits to mimic me."

"And while he waits, what are we to do?" demanded Murilo.

"There is naught we can do, except watch him. As long as he is in that chamber, we dare not ascend the stairs. He has the strength of a true gorilla and could easily tear us all to pieces. But he does not need to exert his muscles; if we open that door he has but to tug that rope, and blast us into eternity."

"How?"

"I bargained to help you escape," answered the priest; "not to betray my secrets."

Murilo started to reply, then stiffened suddenly. A stealthy hand had parted the curtains of one of the doorways. Between them appeared a dark face whose glittering eyes fixed menacingly on the squat form in the scarlet robe.

"Petreus!" hissed Nabonidus. "Mitra, what a gathering of vultures this night is!"

The face remained framed between the parted curtains. Over the intruder's shoulder other faces peered — dark, thin faces, alight with sinister eagerness.

"What do they here?" muttered Murilo, unconsciously lowering his voice, although he knew they could not hear him.

"Why, what would Petreus and his ardent young nationalists be doing in the house of the Red Priest?" laughed Nabonidus. "Look how eagerly they glare at the figure they think is their arch-enemy. They have fallen into your error; it should be amusing to watch their expressions when they are disillusioned."

Murilo did not reply. The whole affair had a distinctly unreal atmosphere. He felt as if he were watching the play of puppets, or as a disembodied ghost himself, impersonally viewing the actions of the living, his presence unseen and unsuspected.

He saw Petreus put his finger warningly to his lips, and nod to his fellow conspirators. The young nobleman could not tell if Thak was aware of the intruders. The ape-man's position had not changed, as he sat with his back toward the door through which the men were gliding.

"They had the same idea you had," Nabonidus was muttering at his ear. "Only their reasons were patriotic rather than selfish. Easy to gain access to my house, now that the dog is dead. Oh, what a chance to rid myself of their menace once and for all! If I were sitting where Thak sits — a leap to the wall — a tug on that rope—"

Petreus had placed one foot lightly over the threshold of the chamber; his fellows were at his heels, their daggers glinting dully. Suddenly Thak rose and wheeled toward him. The unexpected horror of his appearance, where they had thought to behold the hated but familiar countenance of Nabonidus, wrought havoc with their nerves, as the same spectacle had wrought upon Murilo. With a shriek Petreus recoiled, carrying his companions backward with him. They stumbled and floundered over each other; and in that instant Thak, covering the distance in one prodigious, grotesque leap, caught and jerked powerfully at a thick velvet rope which hung near the doorway.

Instantly the curtains whipped back on either hand, leaving the door clear, and down across it something flashed with a peculiar silvery blur.

"He remembered!" Nabonidus was exulting. "The beast is half a man! He had seen the doom performed, and he remembered! Watch, now! Watch! Watch!"

Murilo saw that it was a panel of heavy glass that had fallen across the doorway. Through it he saw the pallid faces of the conspirators. Petreus, throwing out his hands as if to ward off a charge from Thak, encountered the transparent barrier, and from his gestures, said something to his companions. Now that the curtains were drawn back, the men in the pits could see all that took place in the chamber that contained the nationalists. Completely unnerved, these ran across the chamber toward the door by which they had apparently entered, only to halt suddenly, as if stopped by an invisible wall.

"The jerk of the rope sealed that chamber," laughed Nabonidus. "It is simple; the glass panels work in grooves in the doorways. Jerking the rope trips the spring that holds them. They slide down and lock in place, and can only be worked from outside. The glass is unbreakable; a man with a mallet could not shatter it. Ah!"

The trapped men were in a hysteria of fright; they ran wildly from one door to another, beating vainly at the crystal walls, shaking their fists wildly at the implacable black shape which squatted outside. Then one threw back his head, glared upward, and began to scream, to judge from the working of his lips, while he pointed toward the ceiling.

"The fall of the panels released the clouds of doom," said the Red Priest with a wild laugh. "The dust of the gray lotus, from the Swamps of the Dead, beyond the land of Khitai."

In the middle of the ceiling hung a cluster of gold buds; these had opened like the petals of a great carven rose, and from them billowed a gray mist that swiftly filled the chamber. Instantly the scene changed from one of hysteria to one of madness and horror. The trapped men began to stagger; they ran in drunken circles. Froth dripped from their lips, which twisted as in awful laughter. Raging, they fell upon one another with daggers and teeth, slashing, tearing, slaying in a holocaust of madness. Murilo turned sick as he watched and was glad that he could not hear the screams and howls with which that doomed chamber must be ringing. Like pictures thrown on a screen, it was silent.

Outside the chamber of horror Thak was leaping up and down in brutish glee, tossing his long hairy arms on high. At Murilo's shoulder Nabonidus was laughing like a fiend.

"Ah, a good stroke, Petreus! That fairly disemboweled him! Now one for you, my patriotic friend! So! They are all down, and the living tear the flesh of the dead with their slavering teeth."

Murilo shuddered. Behind him the Cimmerian swore softly in his uncouth tongue. Only death was to be seen in the chamber of the gray mist; torn, gashed, and mangled, the conspirators lay in a red heap, gaping mouths and blood-dabbled faces staring blankly upward through the slowly swirling eddies of gray.

Thak, stooping like a giant gnome, approached the wall where the rope hung, and gave it a peculiar sidewise pull.

"He is opening the farther door," said Nabonidus. "By Mitra, he is more of a human than even I had guessed! See, the mist swirls out of the chamber and is dissipated. He waits, to be safe. Now he raises the other panel. He is cautious — he knows the doom of the gray lotus, which brings madness and death. By Mitra!"

Murilo jerked about at the electric quality of the exclamation.

"Our one chance!" exclaimed Nabonidus. "If he leaves the chamber above for a few minutes, we will risk a dash up those stairs."

Suddenly tense, they watched the monster waddle through the doorway and vanish. With the lifting of the glass panel, the curtains had fallen again, hiding the chamber of death.

"We must chance it!" gasped Nabonidus, and Murilo saw perspiration break out on his face. "Perhaps he will be disposing of the bodies as he has seen me do. Quick! Follow me up those stairs!"

He ran toward the steps and up them with an agility that amazed Murilo. The young nobleman and the barbarian were close at his heels, and they heard his gusty sigh of relief as he threw open the door at the top of the stairs. They burst into the broad chamber they had seen mirrored below. Thak was nowhere to be seen.

"He's in that chamber with the corpses!" exclaimed Murilo. "Why not trap him there as he trapped them?"

"No, no!" gasped Nabonidus, an unaccustomed pallor tingeing his features. "We do not know that he is in there. He might emerge before we could reach the trap rope, anyway!

Follow me into the corridor; I must reach my chamber and obtain weapons which will destroy him. This corridor is the only one opening from this chamber which is not set with a trap of some kind."

They followed him swiftly through a curtained doorway opposite the door of the death chamber and came into a corridor, into which various chambers opened. With fumbling haste Nabonidus began to try the doors on each side. They were locked, as was the door at the other end of the corridor.

"My god!" The Red Priest leaned against the wall, his skin ashen. "The doors are locked, and Thak took my keys from me. We are trapped, after all."

Murilo stared appalled to see the man in such a state of nerves, and Nabonidus pulled himself together with an effort.

"The beast has me in a panic," he said. "If you had seen him tear men as I have seen — well, Mitra aid us, but we must fight him now with what the gods have given us. Come!"

He led them back to the curtained doorway, and peered into the great chamber in time to see Thak emerge from the opposite doorway. It was apparent that the beast-man had suspected something. His small, close-set ears twitched; he glared angrily about him and, approaching the nearest doorway, tore aside the curtains to look behind them.

Nabonidus drew back, shaking like a leaf. He gripped Conan's shoulder. "Man, do you dare pit your knife against his fangs?"

The Cimmerian's eyes blazed in answer.

"Quick!" the Red Priest whispered, thrusting him behind the curtains, close against the wall. "As he will find us soon enough, we will draw him to us. As he rushes past you, sink your blade in his back if you can. You, Murilo, show yourself to him and then flee up the corridor. Mitra knows, we have no chance with him in hand-to-hand combat, but we are doomed anyway when he finds us."

Murilo felt his blood congeal in his veins, but he steeled himself and stepped outside the doorway. Instantly Thak, on the other side of the chamber, wheeled, glared, and charged with a thunderous roar. His scarlet hood had fallen back, revealing his black misshapen head; his black hands and red robe were splashed with a brighter red. He was like a crimson and black nightmare as he rushed across the chamber, fangs barred, his bowed legs hurtling his enormous body along at a terrifying gait.

Murilo turned and ran back into the corridor and, quick as he was, the shaggy horror was almost at his heels. Then as the monster rushed past the curtains, from among them catapulted a great form that struck full on the ape-man's shoulders, at the same instant driving the poniard into the brutish back. Thak screamed horribly as the impact knocked him off his feet, and the combatants hit the floor together. Instantly there began a whirl and thrash of limbs, the tearing and rending of a fiendish battle.

Murilo saw that the barbarian had locked his legs about the ape-man's torso and was striving to maintain his position on the monster's back while he butchered it with his poniard. Thak, on the other hand, was striving to dislodge his clinging foe, to drag him around within reach of the giant fangs that gaped for his flesh. In a whirlwind of blows and scarlet tatters they rolled along the corridor, revolving so swiftly that Murilo dared not use the chair he had caught up, lest he strike the Cimmerian. And he saw that in spite of the handicap of Conan's first hold, and the voluminous robe that lashed and wrapped about the ape-man's limbs and body, Thak's giant strength was swiftly prevailing. Inexorably he was dragging the Cimmerian around in front of him. The ape-man had taken punishment enough to have killed a dozen men. Conan's poniard had sunk again and again into his torso, shoulders, and bull-like neck; he was streaming blood from a score of wounds; but, unless the blade quickly reached some absolutely vital spot, Thak's inhuman vitality would survive to finish the Cimmerian and, after him, Conan's companions.

Conan was fighting like a wild beast himself, in silence except for his gasps of effort. The black talons of the monster and the awful grasp of those misshapen hands ripped and tore at him, the grinning jaws gaped for his throat. Then Murilo, seeing an opening, sprang and swung the chair with all his power, and with force enough to have brained a human being. The chair glanced from Thak's slanted black skull; but the stunned monster momentarily relaxed his rending grasp, and in that instant Conan, gasping and streaming blood, plunged forward and sank his poniard to the hilt in the ape-man's heart.

With a convulsive shudder, the beast-man started from the floor, then sank limply back. His fierce eyes set and glazed, his thick limbs quivered and became rigid.

Conan staggered dizzily up, shaking the sweat and blood out of his eyes. Blood dripped from his poniard and fingers, and trickled in rivulets down his thighs, arms, and breast. Murilo caught at him to support him, but the barbarian shook him off impatiently.

"When I cannot stand alone, it will be time to die," he mumbled, through mashed lips. "But I'd like a flagon of wine."

Nabonidus was staring down at the still figure as if he could not believe his own eyes. Black, hairy, abhorrent, the monster lay, grotesque in the tatters of the scarlet robe; yet more human than bestial, even so, and possessed somehow of a vague and terrible pathos.

Even the Cimmerian sensed this, for he panted: "I have slain a *man* tonight, not a *beast*. I will count him among the chiefs whose souls I've sent into the dark, and my women will sing of him."

Nabonidus stooped and picked up a bunch of keys on a golden chain. They had fallen from the ape-man's girdle during the battle. Motioning his companions to follow him, he led them to a chamber, unlocked the door, and led the way inside. It was illumined like the others. The Red Priest took a vessel of wine from a table and filled crystal beakers. As his companions drank thirstily, he murmured: "What a night! It is nearly dawn, now. What of you, my friends?"

"I'll dress Conan's hurts, if you will fetch me bandages and the like," said Murilo, and Nabonidus nodded, and moved toward the door that led into the corridor. Something about his bowed head caused Murilo to watch him sharply. At the door the Red Priest wheeled suddenly. His face had undergone a transformation. His eyes gleamed with his old fire, his lips laughed soundlessly.

"Rogues together!" his voice rang with its accustomed mockery. "But not fools together. You are the fool, Murilo!"

"What do you mean?" The young nobleman started forward.

"Back!" Nabonidus' voice cracked like a whip. "Another step and I will blast you!"

Murilo's blood turned cold as he saw that the Red Priest's hand grasped a thick velvet rope, which hung among the curtains just outside the door.

"What treachery is this?" cried Murilo. "You swore—"

"I swore I would not tell the king a jest concerning you! I did not swear not to take matters into my own hands if I could. Do you think I would pass up such an opportunity? Under ordinary circumstances I would not dare to kill you myself, without sanction of the king, but now none will ever know. You will go into the acid vats along with Thak and the nationalist fools, and none will be the wiser. What a night this has been for me! If I have lost some valuable servants, I have nevertheless rid myself of various dangerous enemies. Stand back! I am over the threshold, and you cannot possibly reach me before I tug this cord and send you to Hell. Not the gray lotus, this time, but something just as effective. Nearly every chamber in my house is a trap. And so, Murilo, fool that you are—"

Too quickly for the sight to follow, Conan caught up a stool and hurled it. Nabonidus instinctively threw up his arm with a cry, but not in time. The missile crunched against his head, and the Red Priest swayed and fell facedown in a slowly widening pool of dark crimson.

"His blood was red, after all," grunted Conan.

Murilo raked back his sweat-plastered hair with a shaky hand as he leaned against the table, weak from the reaction of relief.

"It is dawn," he said. "Let us get out of here, before we fall afoul of some other doom. If we can climb the outer wall without being seen, we shall not be connected with this night's work. Let the police write their own explanation."

He glanced at the body of the Red Priest where it lay etched in crimson, and shrugged his shoulders.

"He was the fool, after all; had he not paused to taunt us, he could have trapped us easily."

"Well," said the Cimmerian tranquilly, "he's travelled the road all rogues must walk at last. I'd like to loot the house, but I suppose we'd best go."

As they emerged from the dimness of the dawn-whitened garden, Murilo said: "The Red Priest has gone into the dark, so my road is clear in the city, and I have nothing to fear. But what of you? There is still the matter of that priest in the Maze, and—"

"I'm tired of this city anyway," grinned the Cimmerian. "You mentioned a horse waiting at the Rats' Den. I'm curious to see how fast that horse can carry me into another kingdom. There's many a highway I want to travel before I walk the road Nabonidus walked this night."

www.ingramcontent.com/pod-product-compliance
Lightning Source LLC
LaVergne TN
LVHW041929090826
845145LV00017B/2751

* 9 7 8 1 4 7 3 3 2 2 9 6 7 *